For my grandson
EOIN
and again for Rose

LAND of the

the G

STONEWALL

FOOT H

the Peace

WESTERN GRASSLAND

FARM

4

OHSTERS

enwood

ey

FOOTHILLS

Sorcerer's Cave

<MOUNTAINS

ls

cul Forest

Melleron's Cottage

<Village>

ands

5

CHAPTER 1

Dark powers

The high meadow led to the base of a ridge, a slope of coarse grass and crumbling rock. Farther up, the slope rose more steeply, into a forbidding stone wall – where once there had been a dark opening leading into a cave.

An opening that had mysteriously disappeared, like a healed wound.

Yet the space of the cave itself still existed, hidden behind the surface of the stone.

It was also greatly changed – brightened by light from unnatural sources, its dank walls and dirt floor hidden by furnishings and carpets and hangings.

At the centre of the cave, hunched in a high-backed chair, a man in a hooded purple cloak was working magic.

Staring with glittering eyes at a tapestry on one wall, he lifted a skinny hand and muttered a stream of words. At once the tapestry shimmered – but its bright patterns remained unchanged.

The hooded man scowled at it. '*Move*, blast it!' he snarled.

He looked down at an open book on his lap – small but incredibly thick, crammed with unreadably tiny writing. Yet when he touched a page, the writing magically enlarged. Peering, he nodded. 'There,' he muttered. 'I overlooked *that* . . .'

He repeated the words, but also moved one hand in a spiralling motion. And the patterns in the tapestry began to swirl and writhe, ever-changing.

As the hooded man smiled thinly, a large shaggy mass stirred at the back of the cave, rising to its feet. A monstrous creature, covered in thick black hair, yellow eyes glowing in the unnatural light.

'Are you still fooling with that?' the monster growled in a deep hoarse voice.

'I'm not *fooling*,' the hooded man snapped, closing the book. 'I'm improving my surroundings.'

The hairy one yawned, fangs glinting. 'Why? You will be leaving before long.'

'But while I'm here,' the hooded one said stiffly, 'I want it to be pleasant.'

The hairy one grunted impatiently. 'And I want to do something besides watch you decorate a cave. I may visit my homeland . . .'

'No,' the hooded one interrupted. 'That would be an unnecessary risk.'

'You do not tell me *no*,' the hairy one rumbled. 'I do as I like.'

The hooded one glowered. 'Would you endanger our plans just because you're *bored*?' Rising, he tucked the thick book carefully into his cloak. 'As it happens, I think we should now be able to go back to the *forest*. It's been over a month, and everything should have settled down . . .'

'About time!' the hairy one said, baring his fangs in a grin. 'So at last we can punish those two little pests!'

'Indeed,' the hooded one hissed. 'In ways that will benefit both of us. And the boy as well – who will learn what it means to be a slave . . .'

Meanwhile, far away from that hidden cave, two small beings were fleeing for their lives.

One bounded on four sturdy legs, the other soared on delicate wings, as they fled across an eerie plain, barren and deathly beneath a pale moon. And racing close behind them came two pursuers.

The first was huge, yellow-eyed and shaggy, fangs and claws and horns glinting in the moonlight. The second was a shadowy figure in a hooded cloak, sailing magically through the air, bony hands reaching . . .

That pursuit was being watched, from a nearby hilltop, by a boy – small, thin, dark-haired, about twelve years old. His face was twisting, his body quivering as if he wanted to leap down from the hilltop. . . But something held him still.

Even though the two small ones were losing that ghastly race, as their pursuers drew closer.

Then, despairingly, the winged one looked towards him, and shrieked his name – perhaps a hopeless cry for help, perhaps an anguished farewell.

'Melleron! *Melleron!*'

CHAPTER 2

Shadow of fear

Melleron woke with a jolt that almost threw him out of bed, and saw his white-haired grandmother, his Nan – who had been calling him – in the doorway.

'Are you all right, Melleron?' Nan said anxiously. 'You were *moaning* . . .'

'I'm fine,' he mumbled, shivering with a leftover chill from the nightmare. 'Just a bad dream . . .'

Nan relaxed. 'I thought it was stomach-ache or worse. Never mind, there's sunshine and breakfast to chase away bad dreams.'

Leaping up, quickly washing and dressing, Melleron dashed to the kitchen where Nan was waiting with hot pancakes. But still the nightmare – which had troubled him several times before – left a shadow on his mind.

'Nan,' he said, swallowing the last bite of his third pancake, 'do dreams ever show what's going to happen?'

'Some folk say that's so,' the old woman said, 'but I doubt it. Dreams are too muddled and unreal. I reckon if they mean anything at all, they tell a bit about what might be *troubling* us.' She patted Melleron's hand. 'I'm not surprised you're still having nightmares, after what happened not much more than a month ago.'

That helped to push away the shadow of Melleron's dream, and so did working at the everyday chores around the cottage, through the morning. But soon, since it was a humid day in high summer, Nan decided to stop and rest in the shade awhile.

Which left Melleron free to dash away towards the place he loved best of all. The enormous, wild expanse of the Peaceful Forest.

He didn't have far to go, since the cottage stood within the fringes of the forest. And he felt no unease about plunging, alone, into its shadowy depths. Both his grandparents had been foresters – Nan still was, though she had grown a bit shaky – and had taught Melleron a forester's skills, to keep him safe.

Also, the forest held few dangers, for in the olden days all its dangerous beasts had been cleared out, forever. It had happened almost by accident, when people fought and won a war against an army of terrible beings from beyond the Stonewall Mountains. The Monster War.

But as Melleron trotted along a familiar forest path, he wasn't thinking about that ancient battle. He was thinking again about his nightmare, and its cause. For it came out of a time, a month or so before, when he and two unusual friends had fought a small frightful war of their own, in the forest.

Their enemy had been a huge, hairy, ferocious monster named Horrimal, who had come over the mountains to raid and terrorize the human lands. In the Peaceful Forest, Horrimal had threatened Melleron's two friends, and Melleron was caught up with them in deadly danger. Even worse, Horrimal had an ally, a human sorcerer named Saelez, who decided to make Melleron his slave.

But with courage and cleverness and luck, Melleron and his friends defeated their enemies. Horrimal and Saelez fled, and the forest was peaceful again.

In fact, life in general had been better since

then for Melleron. Before that, he and Nan had been quite poor, and were scorned or ignored by most people in the area. But after Horrimal had been driven off, the grateful people raised a large sum of money for Melleron as a reward. And everyone became much friendlier.

So, Melleron thought, that amazing summer turned out to be nearly perfect. Except for the nightmare that he kept having.

And except for the fact that the monster Horrimal and the sorcerer Saelez were still lurking somewhere in the Stonewall Mountains, north of the forest. No doubt full of hatred and fury, and possibly plotting revenge . . .

Yet Melleron seemed to be the only one thinking about that. Just as he was the only one having nightmares. Even his two friends, even Nan, seemed to believe that the monster and the sorcerer had gone for good, and there was nothing more to worry about.

'But they could come *back* . . .' Melleron muttered to himself, on the forest path.

Then he almost jumped out of his shoes

when, with a rustle of twigs, something sprang at him from a thicket while something else whirled down from above.

CHAPTER 3

Shattered peace

The first looked like a living statue – a sturdy
little dog, but made of hard stone. The second
had the wings, claws and smooth scales of a
dragon – but was no bigger than a bush-pigeon,
and a bright, startling pink.

'Are you *talking* to yourself, Melleron?' the
dragon laughed. Her name was Rose, which she
insisted was her colour, too, since she hated *pink*.

'Thinking out loud,' Melleron said. 'I had the
dream again, about you two being chased by
Horrimal and Saelez.'

'Rrrrr,' said the little dog, whose name was

Grit, baring sharp teeth that were actual diamonds. He understood what they said, but spoke only his own language, so only Rose understood him.

'Grit says you should dream about *us* chasing *them*,' Rose told Melleron.

'I don't want to dream about them at all,' Melleron muttered. 'I keep wondering if the dream is a sort of warning.'

'A dream is just a *dream*, pictures in the night,' Rose said firmly. 'Those two are a *long* way away from here.'

Melleron sighed. 'What about your idea of telling the Chief of the monsters what happened? He might *do* something. About Horrimal, anyway.'

Rose waved a wing. 'I may do that, sometime. But I don't think the Chief cares too much what happens *here*. Most monsters don't. Anyway, they're not likely to go *hunting* for Horrimal.'

'Rrrr,' Grit said. 'Rrrr.'

Rose nodded. 'Grit says, why ruin the summer *worrying?*'

He's right, Melleron thought. Especially such

a special summer, the three of them together amid the ever-changing marvels of the forest. Autumn, and the re-opening of the village school, would arrive all too soon.

Firmly, he pushed his worries away. 'What do you want to do, then?' he asked brightly. 'Go back to that vale we were exploring, or find something to eat?'

'Rrrr!' Grit said, wagging a stumpy tail.

'*Eat!*' Rose cried, swirling into the air.

They set off towards one of Rose's favourite places, a grove of silverberry bushes, which always had ripe fruit on their branches any time of year. Along the way they paused by an outcrop of flinty rock, which was Grit's favourite

place. He was made of stone and he ate stone –
and loved a nice bit of flint.

When he had broken off a big chunk with his
diamond teeth, they went on to the silverberry
grove, where Melleron and Rose gobbled the big
juicy berries while Grit gnawed his flint like a
dog with a bone. And after that, they went
wandering, while the forest offered its usual
wonderful variety show.

They watched harelings playing, striped duck
paddling, swarm-beetles marching. They startled
a little bush-cat, which Grit chased up a
cherrynut tree, just for fun. And as usual, they
visited a clearing where an ancient iron-oak tree
lay uprooted, where they watered a tiny seedling
that had sprouted among the torn-up roots of its
mighty ancestor.

At last, as the afternoon shaded into evening,
it was time for Melleron to set off for home –
under a heavy gathering of thunder-clouds,
tinged red by the sunset as if wounded, growling
distantly as if in pain.

And the clouds were still overhead next
morning, like a stifling weight upon the humid

forest, as Melleron went to meet his friends again.

But he failed to find them.

Wondering what had delayed or distracted them, he searched around in their usual places, while the clouds muttered overhead. Still they didn't appear. At midday the storm attacked with torrents of rain, lightning lancing through the gloom. But for Melleron, sheltering under a goldfir tree, the rain was the least of his concerns.

Rose and Grit had never before failed to meet him. And rain never bothered them.

So – where *were* they?

When the downpour stopped and the storm drifted away, Melleron went back to searching, ranging more widely, calling their names. But after another hour or two he fell silent, moving with a forester's quiet step – while within him puzzlement gave way to anxiety, and finally to dread.

By then, ranging into the northern reaches of the forest, he was aware of a weird feeling, all around. The forest had grown still, with an *unnatural* stillness, as if its creatures were holding their breath, silenced by terror. And Melleron had known that feeling before – when the monstrous Horrimal had prowled the forest's shadows . . .

It *can't* be him, Melleron tried to tell himself. It must be something else . . . But a coldness like ice crystals gathered along his spine, despite the humid heat.

Shortly he was toiling up a low hill tangled with wirethorn and hookweed, where the stillness felt heavier as if the very air was gripped by fright. On the crest of the hill he looked across a sweep of open ground, mostly free of

24

trees. Where he saw a scene that was his nightmare come true.

On the far side of that open area, Rose and Grit were fighting a hopeless, losing battle against their most deadly enemies.

CHAPTER 4

Evil victory

Fearless as ever, Grit was leaping and snapping at the monster Horrimal while Rose flew and clawed at the monster's frightful face. And Horrimal, growling like the departed thunder, was kicking savagely at Grit, swatting at Rose.

At the same time the sorcerer Saelez in his hooded cloak was hopping around them, yelling. And lengths of weirdly glowing cord were leaping magically from his hands, seeking to wrap around Rose and Grit. But they were quick and agile enough to dodge both the cords and the sweeping blows of the monster.

In the midst of the battle Saelez reached into his cloak, bringing out a small, oddly thick book. After glancing at a page, the sorcerer lifted his glittering gaze.

'Careful!' he shouted to Horrimal, as the monster slashed furiously at Rose. 'Don't damage that pink skin!'

Instantly Rose whirled. 'Not *pink!*' she shrieked. 'Don't call me *pink!*' And a blazing stream of blue fire erupted from her mouth.

She hadn't breathed dragon-fire before, in the battle, because she could never do it when she *wanted* to. It burst out only when she grew completely berserk with fury.

Fighting Horrimal merely made her fiercely angry – but the hated word *pink* threw her over the edge into an almost crazed, truly blazing rage.

Screeching with shock, Saelez reeled backwards, thrusting the book into his cloak. But then he shouted strange words – and more of the magical cords appeared, weaving themselves into a glowing net.

At once the net wrapped around Rose, one strand looping around her mouth to stifle her flame. As she fell, struggling and raging, Saelez flung another net around Grit, its magic withstanding his strength and his sharp diamond teeth.

Side by side on the grass the two of them lay, helpless, as Horrimal's huge clawed hands reached down to them.

And Melleron leaped from the hilltop in a wild, desperate charge.

He had no chance against Horrimal or Saelez, but he hadn't stopped to think. He simply couldn't stand there while Rose and Grit were trussed up as if for slaughter. Yet he hadn't reached them when Horrimal picked up the two captives and galloped heavily off into the forest. While Saelez, with more words of magic, was suddenly transformed – into the winged shape of a swallow-hawk, which flashed away among the treetops.

So Melleron was left alone on that open

ground – standing as if rooted, pale and trembling. While around him the forest creatures came out of their unnatural stillness, back to their everyday sounds, as if nothing had happened there at all.

He took a step forward, thinking wildly that he might track Horrimal through the forest, hoping to find some way to help . . . Then he whirled fearfully, at the sound of a rustle behind him.

And he stared in bewilderment at the sight of his Nan, hobbling towards him.

'Melleron . . .' she said, almost a gasp.

'Nan!' he said. 'What are you doing here?'

'I've been looking for you . . .' she gasped, moving closer.

Melleron was disturbed to see that she looked shakier than ever, pale and weak and hollow-eyed. 'What's wrong, Nan?' he asked worriedly. 'Are you sick?'

'The heat . . .' she croaked, reaching a

trembling hand towards him. 'I think I've walked too far . . .'

As Melleron hurried to support her, she let her hand fall on his arm. Its grip was oddly firm, despite her weakness. Also, her hair seemed longer and wilder than usual, she was wearing a dark dress he had never seen before, and her eyes seemed to be *glittering* . . .

But just as he put all those details together, it became too late.

The old woman shimmered – and became Saelez the sorcerer, laughing cruelly, clutching Melleron's arm.

CHAPTER 5

Into captivity

'I did well as the old crone, didn't I?' Saelez cackled. 'Even though I only saw her once, a month ago!'

Terrified, Melleron fought to free himself. But Saelez snapped some harsh words – and another glowing magic net wrapped itself around him.

Just as Horrimal crashed back into the clearing, scowling, with Rose and Grit still in his clutches.

'Why did you call me back . . . ?' Horrimal began. But then he saw Melleron, and his scowl became a savage grin. 'The *boy!*' he growled.

'How did you find him?'

'He just came running along,' Saelez smirked. 'I saw him from the air. Perhaps he thought he could help his little friends.'

Horrimal grunted. 'I suppose you want me to carry them all.'

'No, no,' Saelez said airily. 'The swallow-hawk form can take the dragon. She weighs no more than a small bird.' His laughter rasped. 'I thought I'd have to search for the boy – but instead he has come to me, as if he *wants* to be my slave!'

Horrimal scooped up Melleron and Grit, galloping into the forest again, a captive under each arm. For Melleron it brought back a time once before when he was carried off, half-stifled by the monster's matted hair. And around that hairy neck, as before, he saw a green stone on a chain, like a pendant – a magic stone, that Saelez used to speak to Horrimal from afar.

But he seemed to be aware of things – the stone, the monster's rank smell, the glowing net around him – as if from a distance. In his horror and despair he was sliding into a daze, an empty numbness settling on him like a fog.

So through that first terrible day, Melleron's mind was mostly blank. He scarcely felt the ache from Horrimal's grip, or the jolting as the monster loped on over the rough wild land. He hardly noticed when at last they left the forest, starting up across the rugged foothills leading to the Stonewall Mountains. The passage of time itself barely registered on his numbed mind, as that nightmare journey went on, and on.

Through it all the monster seemed untroubled by his burdens. Though he was heavy-footed and far from swift, his pace never slackened, no matter how steep the slope, how rough the footing. By sunset he was entering a deep ravine, a shadowed gap between cliffs that formed a corridor through the mountains. Yet even its darkness failed to slow Horrimal down.

But then, at last, in a twilit gully beyond the ravine, Horrimal came to a halt, and set his captives down. That sudden release – from the monster's grip and the endless movement – jolted Melleron some way back towards awareness. Perhaps also, after so many long hours, the effects of shock and terror were beginning to wear off, his numbing inner fog lifting a little.

So he was able to notice that Grit had somehow wriggled one paw free from the magic net. And when Horrimal turned away from them, Grit reached over to touch Melleron with that paw, its claws like splinters of granite, and growled softly, intensely.

In that moment even more of Melleron's clouded blankness fell away.

He could see the little dog's unflinching courage flaring in his eyes, and he realized that Grit was wordlessly urging him *not* to be crushed by terror and hopelessness – not to let himself give in, or give up.

Slowly Melleron nodded, clutching at whatever shreds of his own courage he could find. 'All right, Grit,' he croaked. 'I'll be all right. Don't worry . . .'

Then he gasped and went still, as Horrimal loomed over them, scooping them up again. But he merely took them to a stream at the edge of the gully, holding their faces down to the icy water so they could drink. He had also found some wild flat-peas, and roughly fed a few to Melleron while Grit gnawed at a flinty pebble.

Melleron slept little during the chill mountain night, feeling stiff and exhausted when Horrimal hoisted them up at daybreak and set off again. But at least he was *aware* of the feeling, no longer lost in empty blankness – although that second day made him almost long for it again. The hours passed with agonizing slowness, as Horrimal clambered across one gravelly slope and narrow ledge and bumpy crest after another. In the end even Grit was silenced by misery.

Until, with startling suddenness, the journey ended.

Horrimal was shambling across a high meadow, towards another rocky ridge, when a patch of the ridge's bare stone suddenly shimmered, then *opened*, like a mouth. A cave-mouth – where Saelez stood, gazing down.

'Welcome,' the sorcerer said with a cackling laugh as Horrimal clambered up into the cave and set his captives down. 'I'm glad you've arrived safely.'

Melleron ignored him, twisting within the net, peering around at the cave's weird and unexpected furnishings, trying to see Rose.

'Looking for a way out?' Saelez laughed. 'Don't bother. We may soon live in a far finer place than this, with many doors, but you will be in my power there as you are here. Believe me, boy – for you, there is *no* escape.'

CHAPTER 6

Sorcerer's cave

Turning away, Saelez murmured a word, and the cave mouth vanished again. And though the cave was lit by magically gleaming spheres, to Melleron the loss of the daylight was like the closing of a tomb.

Horrimal lumbered over to a mat at one side. 'Keep them quiet,' he rumbled. 'I need some rest after that journey.' He settled into a shaggy mass and almost at once began snoring.

Saelez sniffed, then beckoned to Melleron. 'Up you get,' he said, and spoke more harsh words. And Melleron jumped – as the net that bound him disappeared.

Wide-eyed, he got stiffly to his feet. Then the sorcerer spoke again, and a single length of the glowing cord appeared in the air. One end hovered as if fastened to something invisible, while the other end looped itself around Melleron's neck.

'Now you can move about,' Saelez grinned. 'But *slowly*, or you'll be stopped.'

Melleron took a wary step, and the cord went with him, drifting weirdly through the air. Meanwhile Saelez casually picked Grit up, carried him to the back of the cave, and set him down. Next to a tiny huddled figure, also in a net.

'Rose!' Melleron cried. He leaped forward, but instantly the cord around his neck jerked him back. Ignoring Saelez's frown, he tried again more slowly, and the trailing cord went with him. Bending over Rose, he saw that her fierce blue eyes were dark with misery – and one loop of the magic net was still wound around her mouth, keeping her silent.

Distress for his friend swept away Melleron's

fear. 'She can't *breathe* properly, like that!' he cried, turning to Saelez. 'Or *eat*, either! You'll *kill* her!'

Saelez glared. 'You will use a more respectful tone, slave. And the dragon is quite all right – for now.'

Before Melleron could reply, Saelez hissed a word, and the loop of cord that bound Rose's mouth slid away. She twitched and blinked with relief, panting.

'If I see one flicker of *fire* from her,' Saelez snapped, 'I'll sew her mouth shut!'

From his cloak he brought out the amazingly thick little book that Melleron had glimpsed before, flicked a page or two, then spoke a phrase. And the nets around Rose and Grit began weirdly to expand – becoming the bars of small glowing *cages*, with room for their captives to stand and stretch.

'Is that better, little soft-heart?' Saelez said sarcastically to Melleron. 'Now – what do they eat?'

'Rose eats fruit,' Melleron said flatly. 'And Grit eats stone.'

Saelez cackled again. 'At least *he'll* be easy to cater for.'

He turned back to the book, then intoned more words. And an earthenware bowl full of marsh-plums and silverberries appeared, on the table at the centre of the cave.

'You feed them,' Saelez said airily. 'I have work to do.'

Moving carefully because of the cord holding him, Melleron gathered up the bowl and went back to the two prisoners.

'Thank you,' Rose whispered between bites of fruit. 'I thought I'd *choke* in that net. Or *starve.*'

'You'll feel better now,' Melleron murmured. 'And I'll get a stone for Grit.'

And then Melleron was dragged sprawling backwards by a painful jerk on the magic cord around his neck.

'What're you *muttering* about?' Saelez snarled, glaring.

'Nothing,' Rose said quickly. 'Just trying to keep our spirits up.'

Saelez sneered. 'Are you dispirited? Too bad. But your woes will end soon, little dragon.' His eyes flared. 'When I put an end to *you!*'

'What do you mean?' Melleron demanded anxiously, getting to his feet.

'You will wish you hadn't asked,' the sorcerer

snarled. 'First, I plan to cast a spell that will make the stone dog *love* me, as a dog loves its master. So he will be my loyal, devoted pet and watchdog, my fierce little protector . . .' He snickered evilly. 'Then I'll work a more powerful magic – which will make me *invulnerable*, so no attack, no weapon, can harm me. And *that* spell needs two special ingredients. The skin, and the fresh blood, of a dragon.'

'*No!*' Melleron cried, horrified. 'You *can't!*'

'I can,' Saelez snapped, 'and I will.'

But then Horrimal stirred with a hoarse growl. 'Am I to get no rest?' he rumbled. 'What is all the shouting?'

'I was informing our *guests*,' Saelez hissed, 'what is in store for the small ones.'

Horrimal lurched to his feet, looking eager. 'Are you ready to do it now?'

'No.' The sorcerer's mouth twisted. 'The spells

are still not . . . available.'

Horrimal scowled. 'So how long must I wait around?'

'I've no idea,' Saelez said with a shrug. 'But it will be worth waiting for.' He stared away, dreamily. 'And afterwards we will return to the human lands. Where you can go on with your private war against the people, while I build my palace and begin my new life – an invulnerable lord, whose bidding must be obeyed . . .'

Horrimal yawned hugely. 'I know all that. And I want to watch you do those magics to the little pests. But I am weary of this cave. I will go out now, to sleep in the sun. And later, I think I will go north to my homeland, after all. To bring my friends to join me, in what you call my "private war".'

Saelez looked disapproving. 'Have you forgotten that when you were last in the land of the monsters, your Chief put you in *chains?* And I had to rescue you?'

'I can stay clear of the Chief and his followers,' Horrimal rumbled. 'And I will be back soon. Open the cave.'

'Very well,' Saelez muttered. 'But keep that magic stone around your neck, so I can speak to you.' Then he snapped a sharp word, and the cave opened.

Staring out longingly at the sunlight, Melleron felt a small surge of hope as the monster tramped away. We're still trapped, he thought, but one enemy is better than two. All we need now is some sort of chance . . .

CHAPTER 7

Passing time

Some days later, far to the south of the cave, Melleron's Nan was in the village that lay some miles away from her cottage, sitting with tears in her eyes in the home of a kindly, grey-haired man – Judge Aldin, leader of the village council.

'Melleron *could* still be in the forest, maybe hurt or something,' Nan was saying. 'But I've looked and looked. And I keep thinking about that monster, and Saelez . . .' She choked back a sob. 'Remember, Saelez was driven out of these lands because he *stole children!* What if he's stolen my boy?'

Aldin sighed. 'It's a terrible thought.'

'So can't you help me, judge?' Nan pleaded. 'And some of the village men?'

'I'm sorry,' the judge said gently. 'Finding a lost boy in the mountains would be nearly impossible. Finding a sorcerer who wants to stay hidden would *certainly* be so. And not many people would want to go that close to the land of the monsters.'

'Then what am I to do?' Nan sobbed.

Aldin patted her hand. 'I'm sorry. I know how hard it is to lose a loved one . . .'

A day or two later, in a wild valley far to the north, two very different beings were talking – chatting comfortably, as friends do. Although neither of them was human.

One was slim and sleek, covered in brown fur with lighter patches, like a big upright cat. But a cat with huge smooth *wings*, folded gracefully.

She was sitting in a marble-elm tree – where she lived, in a large nest formed from its woven branches. And she was talking with a neighbour, who lived in a nearby wood. Which was suitable, since he looked like a thorn tree – a tall thin body and skinny arms and legs, covered in greenish skin like bark and long sharp spikes.

'Are you sure it was Horrimal you saw, Orani?' the thorny one was asking in a thin sharp voice.

'I'm surprised he'd dare to come back.'

'It was Horrimal,' the winged one said. 'Large as life and twice as ugly. But he's a long way from here – down near our southern borders.'

The thorny one shook his head, coarse hair rattling like twigs. 'What's he up to? The Chief will be livid.'

'The Chief's always livid about something, Poljon.' The winged one laughed, a purring growl. 'But he's not likely to bother starting a *search* down there. Though things might get exciting if Horrimal comes back *here*.'

'That would suit me,' the thorny one said. 'Horrimal might be just what we need to keep from having a boring summer . . .'

For Melleron, those first days of captivity had been surprisingly quiet. It seemed that a sorcerer's slave had really very little to *do*. Chores and domestic work were easily managed by Saelez's magic. Even their food – a variety of delicacies, for which Melleron had little appetite – simply appeared on the table, magically.

So Melleron spent much of his time in

idleness, feeling a mixture of boredom and dread. But at least he was still allowed to feed Rose and Grit in their cages. And they both remained undaunted, which lifted his spirits.

Also, Saelez still seemed unable to carry out his evil plan for his small captives. He had told Horrimal before, mysteriously, that the spells weren't 'available' – and somehow they still weren't. Which made Melleron deeply glad.

Besides, he told himself, idleness was better than being overworked, in his slavery. So he stayed quiet, trying not to be noticed – while Saelez spent much of his time poring endlessly over his strange thick book, scribbling and mumbling. In fact Saelez *praised* Melleron, once or twice, for being 'untroublesome'.

And that was perhaps what led Saelez, one day, to decide that he disliked the magic cord that was still looped around Melleron's neck. 'You look like a donkey, with a halter,' the sorcerer cackled. So – after a quick look into his book – he spoke two weird words, and the cord vanished.

Then, as Melleron rubbed his neck with relief,

Saelez smirked. 'We might enjoy some fresh air as well,' he said, and spoke another word.

And the front of the cave opened wide.

CHAPTER 8

Obedient slave

Melleron could hardly believe his eyes. It was a
dull day outside, with drizzly rain, but it looked
quite wonderful. And Saelez was turning
carelessly away, leaving him by the open cave-
mouth. With nothing at all holding him back.

Heart pounding, Melleron poised himself for
an all-out, break-neck sprint towards freedom.
But he didn't move.

For one thing, he couldn't run off and desert
Rose and Grit. But also he saw that while Saelez
was moving away as if unconcerned, his head
was slightly turned. He's *watching* me, Melleron

realized. He *expects* me to run. And his magic would stop me after the first step.

So – though every bit of his being was screaming with the urge to run – he let his head droop, and turned to follow Saelez.

The sorcerer looked startled. 'You surprise me,' he said, smiling. 'I was sure you'd run – though that would have proved quite pointless, and painful for you. Perhaps you've realized you're better off here, with me. Well done, Melleron.'

The praise made Melleron feel even more miserable. He could hardly look at Rose and Grit later, when he fed them. So he was amazed when Rose praised him too.

'You did *exactly* right, Melleron,' she announced through a mouthful of berries. 'It's *very* clever, making him think well of you.'

'Is it?' Melleron asked, surprised.

'Very,' she told him. 'He is growing more at *ease* with you, less watchful. He has already taken off that cord, giving you free run of the cave. If he gets more off-guard, you might have a chance to get away . . . !'

'From his magic?' Melleron sighed. 'Not likely.'

Rose's eyes flashed. 'There are *always* chances, Melleron, there is *always* hope. For all his power, Saelez is still human, and humans have *weaknesses*. Watch him – and if you see a chance, *take* it! If you could get away, you could bring *help* . . .'

'Rrrr,' Grit said encouragingly.

'I don't know where I'd find help,' Melleron said dismally. 'And I still can't imagine how I'd escape Saelez's magic. Or if I'd have the nerve to try . . .'

'You were brave and quick and clever *before*,' Rose snapped, 'when we defeated Horrimal. You must be *again*. Go on making Saelez pleased with you, and stay alert, and never, *never*, give up hope!'

Over the following day or so Melleron took those words to heart, and did as she said. And as Saelez grew more pleased with him, he finally realized *why* it was that the sorcerer wanted a slave.

Not to be a servant or a victim, but to be someone to talk to when he wished. And, most especially, someone to *show off* to.

During that first evening after Melleron's halter had been removed, Saelez had spent time as usual poring over his strange book, muttering to himself. But he grew friendly and chatty over supper – talking about the food, the exotic dishes he might magically provide. While Melleron made himself listen politely and murmur 'yes, sir' now and then.

At last Saelez paused, smiling thinly. 'Are you truly interested in the working of magic, Melleron?'

'Yes, sir, I am,' Melleron replied, which was true enough. Melleron found magic itself fascinating. It was Saelez's *use* of it that was evil.

The sorcerer nodded. 'I should show you more. You've only seen simple bits and pieces – and a few upsetting spells, earlier . . .'

As he thought about those 'upsetting' magics, such as the capture of Rose and Grit, a shadow darkened Melleron's eyes. And Saelez saw it, but misunderstood.

'You mustn't be afraid,' he smiled. He leaned closer. 'Why – I might even let you cast a spell *yourself!*'

'*Me?*' Melleron cried, astonished.

'Certainly,' Saelez smirked. 'Of course for any major spells you would need some natural ability, along with years of study and special preparation. But *anyone* can perform a *simple* spell – with this.'

And then, even more astonishingly, he brought out the mysterious book from his cloak, and casually handed it to Melleron.

Melleron almost dropped it, for it was not only incredibly thick but unexpectedly heavy, covered in shiny leather that felt cold and slippery. Opening it carefully, he blinked at the dark writing that crowded the pages, too impossibly tiny to read.

But when his fingers touched a page, it suddenly, shockingly enlarged, so every word was clear.

Then Saelez reached over and took the book away. 'It's a *spell-book*, made by a group of master-wizards. I . . . *acquired* it from my own teacher, just before he died. It contains thousands and thousands of spells, big and small . . .' He turned a few pages, then handed the book back to Melleron. 'There, at the top of the left-hand page. A nice easy magic, only one word. Try it.'

The word was strange and hard to say, but on his second try Melleron got it right. And he nearly fell off his chair – for on the table before him appeared a small but perfect cake, glazed with melted sugar.

Saelez cackled merrily at the look on his face. 'Well done! Now you too are a sorcerer! And you may eat the cake – it's quite real . . .'

Warily Melleron took a bite, which seemed perfectly normal and delicious. But as he ate, he was staring at the spell-book. What if I could find a magic, he thought excitedly, that would help Rose and Grit and me *escape* . . . ?

CHAPTER 9

Pages of sorcery

'What are you thinking?' Saelez asked, reaching for the book again. 'That you'd like to turn yourself into a whistle-fly and buzz away?'

'Oh, no, sir,' Melleron said, trying to look innocent.

'Anyway, you couldn't,' Saelez told him. 'To be a *shape-changer*, a sorcerer must undergo many rigorous, dangerous rituals, over a long time. Only then will the spells work when he speaks them.' He smirked. 'Not every student of magic can face that preparation. But I did – and I am something of a *master* of shape-changing.'

He had been turning pages in his book as he spoke. Glancing down with a twisted grin, he spoke a rasping sentence. Then he was gone – and in his place sat a giant slavering howler-bear.

Surprise as much as fright made Melleron fling himself back with a cry, almost overturning his chair. And the bear became Saelez again, laughing gleefully.

'You're a fearful little one, aren't you?' he cackled. 'Did you think you were about to be eaten?' And he laughed and laughed, as Melleron tried to smile.

Over the next day or so, it became Saelez's favourite entertainment – sudden shape-changes, to frighten Melleron. At any moment Melleron might find himself face to face with a snarling blood-wolf, an oversized spider-bat, perhaps a grinning skeleton or a blood-drenched headless ghost.

And every time he followed Rose's advice about playing up to Saelez, and pretended to be terrified, since the sorcerer seemed to enjoy his fear so much.

Meanwhile, he carefully watched Saelez's every move whenever he brought out his spell-book. If we're ever to get any sort of chance, he kept thinking, it might come from the book. And Rose agreed – though neither she nor Melleron could work out how to get past the fact that Saelez always kept the book safe.

'Never mind,' Rose told him. 'Thanks to you, we have *much* more hope now than we had before. Keep on as you are, Melleron, and *something* will turn up.'

So Melleron went on being a humble slave and a good audience, biding his time. And learning more about the spell-book.

'The book has its own peculiar magics,' Saelez

told him, at the table one evening. 'The way its pages enlarge, for instance. And it's *indestructible* – it can't be torn up or burned or anything. But also, although there are thousands of spells in it, as I told you, they aren't always the *same* spells!'

Spells constantly *vanished* from the book, he explained, and were replaced – by others that had vanished before, perhaps long before, making a reappearance. And no one ever knew when a spell might vanish, or when it might come back.

'That's why I'm still waiting,' Saelez grumbled, 'to deal with your little friends.' He scowled at the spell-book, setting it on the table. 'The spells that I plan to use on them have vanished from the book, and haven't yet reappeared.'

Good, Melleron thought. 'Why does the book do that, sir?' he asked.

'The wizards who made the book probably found it amusing,' Saelez sniffed. 'But also in that way the book can contain an *enormous* number of spells and still be small enough to carry around. All in all, there are more than a *million* spells in it – but only a few thousand are actually *there* at any one time, do you see? Yet it's quite thick and heavy enough just with those.'

'Couldn't you have more than one book?' Melleron asked carefully.

Saelez shook his head gloomily. 'The magic won't allow copies of any sort. I do keep writing out important spells, and also trying to commit them to memory, in case they disappear from the book. But it's no good. Written copies last awhile – often for days – but then, without fail, they start to fade, and soon vanish. Forever.' He sighed. 'And copies of *copies* fade more quickly. While spells linger in the *memory* for only a few hours, before they are forgotten . . .'

Melleron's eyes widened as the realization struck him. If Saelez lost the book, before long he would lose all his magical power! If only, he thought. If only . . .

'Still,' the sorcerer said, as if echoing his thought, 'as long as the book is close to hand' – he smiled nastily – 'I can *refresh* my memory of certain spells . . .'

The smile was just enough warning. Snarling

an ugly phrase, Saelez abruptly changed himself into an oversized, hissing fen-lizard. Melleron shrieked and cowered in pretended terror, crumpling his face as if about to burst into tears.

Saelez reappeared, laughing delightedly. 'Poor little faint-heart – am I being unkind? Don't cry. I'll become something *nice* for you. Something harmless and lovely . . .'

Flicking through the spell-book, he spoke another few words, and changed again. Into a broad-winged, brilliantly coloured paint-box butterfly. The gorgeous creature fluttered over the table, as if showing off its colours . . .

And without thought or hesitation, Melleron snatched up a heavy soup ladle and smashed the butterfly out of the air.

CHAPTER 10

Running north

As the insect dropped limply towards the floor it
turned back into Saelez, landing with a crash,
unconscious and sprawled, breathing raggedly.
And Melleron whirled, snatched up the spell-
book and sprang to Rose and Grit.

'What's *happened?*' Rose cried, since they
couldn't see from the back of the cave.

Melleron explained in a rush, frantically
turning the pages of the book, looking for a spell
that would release them. Desperately hoping it
would be the one that Saelez had used to remove
the cord from his neck.

Because, although he couldn't remember that spell itself, he *did* remember that it was quite near the front of the book . . .

'We need the magic that opens the *cave*, too,' Rose said anxiously.

'I know,' Melleron gasped. Then he stopped, stiffening. 'There!' he muttered tensely. 'Now . . .'

He took a deep breath, then spoke two long words, a series of harsh sounds.

And nothing happened.

'Hang on,' Melleron muttered. 'I think I said it wrong . . .' And he spoke the words again, with a different tone in the last syllable.

Instantly, the glowing cages vanished, as if they had never been.

All three of them cried out in relief and triumph. But as they fled across the cave, they paused to inspect Saelez – still sprawled and unconscious.

'Rrr, rrr,' Grit growled fiercely.

'Grit says it's too bad he's not still a *butterfly*,' Rose said. 'Then we could *squash* him, finish him off for *good*.'

Melleron looked faintly sick. 'I don't think I could do that.'

'No,' Rose agreed. 'And we can't kill him as he is, in cold *blood*.'

'Let's just get away,' Melleron said. Going back to the book, turning a few more pages, he found the single magic word he needed. Carefully, he spoke it.

The cave-mouth opened, revealing a soft summer twilight, with a gentle breeze.

'You're getting *good* at magic, Melleron,' Rose laughed as they raced away down the slope and across the meadow.

'It's the spell-book, not me,' Melleron panted,

cramming the book inside his shirt as he ran.

'It's your magic if you're *doing* it,' Rose pointed out. 'And won't Saelez lose his power, now, without the book?'

'Not right away,' Melleron said. 'No one can *remember* spells for long, but he has *copies* of a lot of spells. He said that written copies don't fade away for some days.'

'Rrrrr,' Grit said.

'Right,' Rose agreed. 'That means if he isn't badly hurt, he could still turn into a *hawk* or something, and come after us. We'd better keep on without *stopping* tonight, to get as far away as we can before sun-up.'

Melleron frowned. 'And there's Horrimal too. He and Saelez are both likely to chase us, all the way back to the Peaceful Forest.'

'Rrr,' Grit growled.

'Yes,' Rose said quietly. 'That's why we're not *going* back there.'

By then they had crossed the meadow and were moving up a gravelly slope – where Melleron stopped, staring at Rose through the twilight. 'Not *going* . . . ?'

'Not yet,' Rose said. 'We can't just keep *running*. We have to find a way to get free of Saelez and Horrimal for *good*. And for that we need *help*.'

'Where from?' Melleron asked weakly, though he thought he knew the answer.

'From our Chief, and our friends, who'd be able to handle Horrimal and possibly Saelez too, if they wanted to,' Rose said. 'So we have to go *north*, Melleron. To the land of the monsters.'

As they hurried on along a high ridge, Melleron fell silent, thinking uneasily about the fearful land they were heading for. Rose always said that many of its monsters were friendly – but he kept thinking about the others. . .

Also, he was silent to save breath. Grit's stony strength was tireless, but Rose's slim wings soon grew weary, and Melleron was worn out by the evening's dramas. Yet they dared not stop, even when the ridge led to a series of rugged slopes, with treacherous drops half-hidden in the moonlight. So as the hours passed Melleron became more and more exhausted, stumbling blindly along behind Grit.

And he nearly fell on his face when the little dog suddenly stopped with a growl – while Rose hissed softly and drifted higher into the air.

Blinking, Melleron saw the glassy-grey light of dawn in the east. And they were on an easy slope that was taking them *downwards*, into a leafy vale.

Of course Horrimal had brought them through the worst of the mountains, to the cave. And now, Melleron realized, they had come most of the rest of the way – down from the cruel cliffs and ridges, on to the gentler, greener northern foothills.

But why had they stopped? And then through his weariness Melleron heard what his friends had heard. Rough, harsh, growling voices, not far away.

'*Monsters,*' Rose said, swirling down. 'I'll go and look.'

As she soared away, the growling voices seemed to draw nearer – then suddenly became a burst of loud roaring, making Melleron jump. Had Rose been seen? He could also hear heavy crashing and crackling in the brush . . . But those sounds quickly began to fade, as if the monsters were rushing off the other way.

After a time that seemed to last forever, Melleron jumped again when Grit growled. But he was wagging his stubby tail – as Rose came swooping down on to a bush.

'It was *Horrimal*,' she said breathlessly. 'With that *gang* of his – headed south. I think they spotted me . . . One of them must have *very* good eyes . . .'

'Saelez must be all right, then,' Melleron said gloomily. 'He must have called Horrimal back, with that magic stone.'

'Horrimal could be going south for his *own* reasons,' Rose pointed out. 'Anyway, I led them in the wrong direction for a way, then I *lost* them. We should be safe enough if we keep on for a while.'

Nearly an hour later, when Rose was sure that they had left the gang of monsters far behind, she had another idea. 'What about *magic*, Melleron?' she asked. 'Could you find a *spell* in that book, to hide us?'

'I can look,' Melleron mumbled wearily. 'But there are thousands of spells in the book – it could take ages . . .'

'Never mind, then,' Rose said, yawning daintily. 'We'll hide *ourselves*. No one's after us *now*, and I'm *tired*.'

So they found a cosy thicket and slept, well hidden and undisturbed. And next day they kept moving, northwards. As they went along Melleron tried looking through the book, for a spell that would hide them. But he found nothing, and soon gave up after twice nearly walking into a tree.

Still, Rose kept careful watch from the air, seeing no signs of pursuit but spotting a butter-apple tree with some early fruit. Rested and fed – there were plenty of pebbles for Grit – they covered a good deal of ground that day. And in the evening they decided against pushing on through the darkness.

'We're in the *clear*,' Rose said, smiling. 'We don't have to wear ourselves out. And *tomorrow*, we'll be in the land of the monsters.'

That made Melleron shiver a little. But by sun-up they were mostly concerned about being hungry, as they set off again. Before long they entered a broad valley, like a giant basin with low hills around it. And Rose swirled in a joyous circle.

'We've crossed the border!' she cried. 'We're home, we're safe, and we can have *breakfast!*' She pointed with a wing. 'Over there, not far, is a *silverberry* grove!' She waved the other wing. 'And over on that hill is a *stony* patch, with flints . . .'

With that Grit went bounding hungrily away. Rose sighed, then laughed. 'You find the berries, Melleron,' she said. 'I'll try to keep Grit from eating the *hillside* . . .'

She swooped away, while Melleron trotted eagerly in the direction she had shown. In that quiet green-clad valley, with the prospect of silverberries making his mouth water, he forgot all his earlier uneasiness. In a few moments he was devouring the big juicy berries just as if he was in his own forest.

And then he heard the scream.

It was a faraway cry, shrill and wild, but he knew it was Rose's voice. It froze him rigid, with a berry half-way to his mouth. Then he jerked, dropping the berry, hearing slightly fainter sounds, fierce and rough, like some he had heard not long before.

The growling and roaring of monsters.

CHAPTER 11

Alone

The terror that gripped him suddenly released him, like a bowstring releasing an arrow. In a headlong sprint he raced away towards the sounds, in the direction that Rose and Grit had taken. And he was still running at full speed, white-faced and wild-eyed, when he reached a place where the side of a low hill showed a deep cleft, bright with flinty stone.

It was silent, deserted – but he knew it was where Grit and Rose had been, where the terrible sounds had come from. He didn't need a forester's skills to read the clear and dreadful signs. Torn-up turf, broken bushes, scarred earth with marks of huge clawed feet, a splash of blood . . .

Rose and Grit had been attacked by monsters, and had lost the unequal battle.

Dazed by horror, Melleron roamed the area, looking for some sign of hope. And he was crouched by another blood-smear, desperately hoping it wasn't Rose's, when he glimpsed a *movement*, on top of the low hill.

With fright flaring through him he dropped behind a low bush, peered up through the leaves – and saw a monstrosity. A tall, upright, bulky creature with lumpy purple skin, red eyes and a blunt muzzle filled with jagged teeth.

The monster half-turned, glancing back. 'Thought I saw something,' he growled.

And
five other frightful
creatures loomed up on to
the hilltop, staring down.

One of them had thick plates of
grey hide like armour, and growths
like daggers along his spine. The
second was squat and hairless,
with dead-white skin, extra-long
teeth and a spiny ruff. The third
was small and scaly with hooked
claws and bulging eyes. The
fourth was as huge and shaggy as
Horrimal, but without horns and
with thick brown hair, not black.

And the fifth was Horrimal himself.

'What was it?' he rumbled.

'Something moving,' the tall purple one said.

'The boy!' Horrimal growled. 'I knew he
would be nearby . . .'

77

The armoured one grunted. 'Any human youngster would run like crazy the other way, if he heard the noise we were making.'

'Maybe not this one,' Horrimal growled. 'Come and look around.'

And the five of them started down the hillside.

Every bit of Melleron wanted him to scream and run. But instead, calling on his forest instincts, he slid silently away through the tall grass, slipping from bush to bush.

Behind him he could hear the monsters growling as they searched around where he had been seen. And when he looked back from behind a small goldfir, he saw the six of them moving in his direction.

They also seemed to be arguing – and Horrimal had the last word. 'It will not hurt us to keep looking,' he growled, his words clear to Melleron. 'Saelez will reward us, if we find him . . .'

Melleron nearly collapsed in fresh panic. Saelez *must* be alive and unhurt. And Horrimal and the others could have met him in the mountains, to begin their pursuit.

So Saelez might be somewhere close by, vengefully searching . . .

Behind him, the six horrors had fanned out, tramping forward in a widespread line, searching a broad sweep of land. If he moved sideways, to try to slip past them, he might be spotted. And he couldn't hide and hope to stay unseen as they went past. He had to stay ahead of them. Which meant going *north*.

He didn't want to go that way. Rose had hoped to get help from the Chief of the monsters, but Melleron doubted whether the Chief would help *him*. Even if he knew where to find the Chief, or had the nerve to ask.

Yet he had no choice. He was being *driven* northward.

Shivering, terrified, desperately alone, he crept away like a hunted animal, deeper into the heart of that inhuman land.

The strange slow hunt went on through the day, farther and farther across the valley.

The spread-out line of the monsters advanced

steadily, peering under every shrub, watching all around. And Melleron went on creeping behind bushes, slithering through grass, unable to hurry, fearful of making a twig snap or a branch thrash.

Even so, by mid-afternoon he had drawn well ahead of them. So he relaxed a little, worn down by tension and weariness. And so he made a slip – stumbling against a lady-birch sapling, which bent and flailed.

Behind him he heard a faint shrill cry. *'There! There he is!'*

Crouching, staring back, Melleron saw the monsters – looking small at that distance –

beside a lofty orchid-tree. With another smaller shape high in the treetop, which he realized was the scaly one with the bulging eyes. Sharp, long-sighted eyes that had spotted the sapling's movement.

At once the monsters charged forward, the scaly one whisking down the tree and following. But Melleron scrambled away, weariness forgotten, straining not to make any more giveaway mistakes. So he kept his distance, ahead of them.

But fresh panic was gathering in him. He was managing to hide from them and stay ahead of them, but they were far stronger, and would be able to keep coming all day and all night. And what if some of them could see like cats in the dark? What if he made more mistakes, as he grew more tired?

He needed to get clear of them, to find a hideaway where he could rest. But the valley's scattered brush and long grass would not provide it.

And then, as the afternoon wore on, he snaked through the grass to the top of a low rise, and saw a broad dark band like a wall, in the distance ahead. Which nearly made him whoop with joy.

A *forest*. At least a big expanse of woodland, looking wonderfully thick and dense. He could hide from a hundred monsters, in there.

He crept on, smiling slightly. And while he was safely hidden in the woodland, he thought, he could go on looking for a special way not only to hide but to *escape*. A magic way, using the spell-book.

CHAPTER 12

Magical mist

At about the same time, far to the south, a lonely figure was plodding along a path in the Peaceful Forest. Melleron's Nan, weary and drawn, spending another day in the forest, as she did every day. Searching.

She had found no sign of Melleron, in any of the forest's secret ways and places. She knew it was most likely that Melleron had been carried off, to the mountains or beyond. Yet she kept on, searching the forest.

She did so because she clung to a tiny hope that he *might* be there. And because she couldn't simply sit in her cottage and do nothing.

And she would go on, the next day, and the next . . . As long as she was able . . .

Meanwhile, far to the north, the strange being like a thorn tree was standing among spiky bushes, picking bristle-pears, when his cat-like winged friend settled gracefully on to the turf beside him.

'Orani!' he said brightly. 'What's the gossip?'

The winged one smiled. 'You'll like this, Poljon. You know those five bone-heads who always hung around with Horrimal? They've gone off to *join* him.'

'So Horrimal's recruiting,' the thorny one said thoughtfully. 'He must be planning something interesting . . .'

'You never know,' the winged one said. 'Anyway, the Chief's in a temper again.'

'Is he going to do anything?' the thorny one asked.

'He's talking about going south for a look,' the winged one said. 'But it may be just talk.

Still, *I* might fly back down there, and sniff around.'

'Mm,' the thorny one said. 'I might go myself. The Greenwood there is lovely.' He grinned. 'And why should we let Horrimal have all the fun?'

And also about the same time, back in the valley where Melleron was being hunted, a fierce-eyed swallow-hawk swooped down into a sheltered clearing. Where Horrimal and the other monsters were lolling in the late-afternoon sun, with scraps of food scattered on the turf, and a large cloth sack lying on one side.

The hawk landed, shimmered, and became the cloaked figure of Saelez – with a strip of cloth around his head like a bandage, his eyes glittering furiously.

'Well?' he snapped at Horrimal. 'When we spoke through the magic stone, you said you had found the boy! Where is he?'

Horrimal waved a huge hand. 'Up ahead somewhere. Not far.'

'Then why are you lying around *here?*' Saelez almost shrieked.

'Resting,' Horrimal rumbled. 'We have been searching all day.'

'The boy's got to be worn out too, by now,' the purple monster added.

Saelez snorted. 'The boy is very capable in the wilds, as you should know by now. He could be getting even farther ahead!'

'Then go look for him,' said the bulging-eyed one, sniggering.

'I intend to,' Saelez fumed. 'And I expect the lot of you to do the same. Before nightfall, I want him in my hands!'

Shortly afterwards, Melleron entered the woodland, which was every bit as dense and overgrown as he had hoped. Knowing that the monsters had fallen farther behind, he went a little deeper, then paused – to look further through the spell-book, still hoping to find a simple spell, easily managed, that would hide him magically.

But with all the thousands of spells in the bulky little book, he spent a long, edgy time flicking through the pages, finding nothing of use. Growing nervous, after having glanced through nearly half of the book, he was ready to give up – until he turned over a few more pages, and saw a few short lines. A magic recipe for a Cloud of Safe-keeping.

Reading it swiftly, he saw that the spell needed simply a selection of herbs, fresh water to moisten them, a plain pattern drawn on the ground, and a few words. No more. Almost laughing out loud, he went to work.

The herbs were common ones, growing all around. When he had gathered enough, he found a brook nearby and moistened them as required. Then, in a hollow beneath some leafy trees, he drew a long oval shape on the ground and scattered the wet leaves around its edge. Finally, he stepped into the oval, peering at the book through the dimness – as the afternoon waned towards sunset – and read out the words.

At once the wet leaves began to steam gently. As the steam rose, it thickened into a mist. The Cloud of Safe-keeping, gathering around him like a veil.

Just like any other patch of mist, he thought, that might form in a shaded hollow. Taking a chance, he stepped out of the oval – but the mist stayed still, looking as perfectly ordinary as he hoped. Also, while he had been able to see dimly through it from *inside*, it seemed thicker from the outside, so that everything within the oval was entirely hidden.

Sighing with relief and weariness, Melleron crept back into the mist, pulling leaves together for a bed, while sunset drew an extra veil of darkness around him.

CHAPTER 13

Terror in the woods

It seemed only a moment before birdsong woke him into a sunlit morning. The mist-cloud around him looked a little ragged, as if it might not last much longer, but all else was peaceful. Moving away, he crept back to the edge of the woods and gazed across the valley.

The pursuing monsters had clearly also stopped for the night, for their dark shapes were still quite distant. But still hunting . . . still advancing . . .

Good, he thought, drawing back into the greenery. They were definitely heading towards the woods, and should arrive before long. And when they had arrived, he could start circling safely through the dense cover, doubling back past them, and be away – southward – before they knew he'd turned.

And then, somehow, he would try to find out what had happened to his friends.

Drifting back into the deep woods, he found a patch of wild sweetbeans and had breakfast, feeling almost at ease. He was at home in the woodland, he was far less exposed there, and now he had his magic mist to protect him as well.

But did he? Suddenly chilled, he remembered that spells could *vanish* from the spell-book, without warning . . . Snatching the book from inside his shirt, he saw with relief that the mist-spell hadn't vanished. Still, it *might*, any time. And he *needed* it – especially to get himself back across the valley.

The anxiety stayed with him through the morning as he waited for the monsters to reach the woods. At midday, he was crouching in a cluster of lady-birch trees, still waiting – when the sight of the birches' loose peeling bark jogged his memory.

Of Saelez, in the cave, endlessly *copying out* important spells.

Quickly pulling away a length of birch-bark, he found a sharp-pointed twig, and wrote out the mist-spell – scratching the letters deeply into the soft smooth bark.

He knew from Saelez that copied-out spells faded away, in time, though not as soon as remembered ones. And while he could write it out again, whenever it started to fade from the bark, he also knew that *copies* of copies faded even more rapidly.

But having the copy made him feel better. And if the precious spell did vanish from the book, the copy might last long enough to get him across the valley.

On impulse, because there was room on the bark, he also copied out the two other small magics that he had used before – the brief spell that had got rid of the glowing cords, and the one word that had conjured the little cake. He even tried that one again, and the cake that appeared was just as tasty as the first one.

When he was done, he rolled up the piece of bark and slid it down into his sock, so it wouldn't be lost or crumpled. Then he moved off, for a drink at a small clear spring that he had spotted earlier. Clumps of bread-root plants grew by the spring, and he was happily digging some up – when he heard a voice.

A monstrous voice, frighteningly near. Not Horrimal's rumble, but weirdly hollow and booming.

'I really *hate* all this trudging around,' the voice was saying. 'When we find that wretch, wherever he's hiding, I'm going to make him *suffer.*'

Melleron slid noiselessly aside, into a low

trench hidden in tangleweed, just in time.

Seven frightful monsters – which he had never seen before – were marching towards the spring, towards him.

He saw a shaggy one and a scaly one, a bulky one and a bony one, a dark one who looked like an insect, and a pale one who looked like a fungus. But he was staring most fearfully at the one in the centre, who had the booming voice. That one was immense, twice as tall as any of the others, with *four* huge arms – along with long thick trailing yellow hair, and giant dagger-sharp tusks.

Then Melleron flattened himself, wriggling deeper into the weed, at the sound of a new voice – from *above*. And a cat-like monster with wide smooth wings circled down to land.

'Haven't seen a thing,' the winged one announced. 'But it's not easy to search woodland from the air.'

'It's no easier searching down here,' the four-armed giant grumbled. 'Do you think he has left the woods? We could be wasting our time . . .'

'I would have seen him, out in more open country,' the winged one said. 'No, he's in here somewhere. We'll find him.'

'Soon, I hope,' the giant one boomed. 'Because I'm getting *really* annoyed. I'm beginning to think I might just rip his *head* off.'

In that moment, as Melleron huddled in the weeds trying not to tremble, another flash of terror clutched at him. A short distance away, he saw a bird move slightly on a branch. A bird that seemed to be *hiding*, among the leaves, watching the monsters.

A swallow-hawk.

CHAPTER 14

Circling away

The hawk's yellow eyes held a unnatural glitter – and a swallow-hawk was Saelez's favourite shape, for travelling . . .

Melleron stared at it, frozen, as a trapped hareling looks at a real hawk. But then the monsters tramped off, soon out of sight among the trees, and the hawk in turn spread its wings and flew away. And before long Melleron crept out of the weeds and fled as well.

He kept an extra-careful watch, as he went along, for he had no doubt that *he* was the one the new monsters were seeking. Who else was being hunted in those woods? So those horrors had to be more of Horrimal's gang.

Still, though he moved around all morning – stealthily, quiveringly alert – he had no further glimpses of monsters or swallow-hawks. Pausing for a rest at midday, he played safe by summoning his mist again – finding the spell still unchanged in the book, and also still clear, with the others, on the roll of bark hidden in his sock.

Safely hidden, paging idly through the book while nibbling some of the bread-roots that he dug up before, he noticed a spell on the very last page – which hadn't been there before. Clearly it was one that had disappeared from the book, previously, and had just reappeared, as spells did. And it was a shock – because it showed how to *destroy* the spell-book.

So the book wasn't indestructible, as Saelez had claimed. And if it was destroyed, Saelez would lose his powers, once his copies faded away as they were sure to do.

But it couldn't happen yet, Melleron thought – not while *he* still needed the book.

And he found that he felt slightly sad about the idea of destroying it at all. It was so exciting and amazing to do even the small magics he could manage. With the added pleasure of using Saelez's own magic book to escape from him and his allies . . .

If I kept the book, he said dreamily to himself, I could try to learn how to do *bigger* spells. I could be – Melleron the Magician!

That made him smile, but not for long. He knew that while he had the spell-book, he would never be safe. Saelez would never stop hunting him, because he would never stop wanting the book.

So, to stop Saelez, he thought, the book would have to be destroyed, before long. But as he read through the spell of destruction he saw that it was hugely difficult – weird and complex, with a long list of unpleasant ingredients . . . And then he peered more closely.

A few added lines, even tinier, gave a 'Swifter Way' to destroy the book.

As he read, Melleron's eyes filled with tears. He might once have been able to use that Swifter

Way, because it required only one special thing. But that was something that he had lost, and might never find again . . .

The sadness stayed with him for the rest of the day. So did tension and fear, because during those hours he decided to start his careful circle that would take him out of the woodland, leaving *all* the crowds of monsters behind. And to avoid being seen or leaving any trace, he had to move very slowly, with extra care, through the thickest undergrowth he could find. Which was what he did, for many hours, circling away one silent step at a time, hardly disturbing a leaf.

At that pace, he knew, he would still be in the woods when night fell. But the mist-spell was still in the book, reassuring him. Indeed, he stopped just after sunset, weary from hours of concentration – finding a narrow gully and making his mist.

Settling into his hideaway, munching another bread-root, he looked at his copied spells on the birch-bark, and cut a few of the words more deeply where they seemed to have started fading a little. Then, with the last of the daylight fading as well, he tucked the bark back into his sock and settled himself to sleep.

Sunrise found him awake, rested and ready for another day of stealthy creeping through the thickets, hiding from the monstrous hunters. Carefully he studied the woods all around, but saw only greenery, heard only birds and insects. So he stepped out of the mist, moving up out of the gully.

Behind him, shattering the stillness, he heard a hiss of astonishment. And a sharp startled voice said, 'What's this? A *boy?*'

He whirled – and saw a *tree* stalking towards him.

Through his terror, Melleron realized it was a monster who looked like a thorn tree, with a narrow greenish body and spindly, spiky limbs. 'Where did you *come* from, boy?' it demanded, reaching out a thorn-clawed hand.

Melleron hurtled frantically away, hearing the thorn-monster cry, 'No – come back!' He raced on, weaving among trees, leaping through brush, until he could run no more. Gasping for breath, he huddled by a huge tree, quivering.

Nothing seemed to be chasing him – but still he felt unnerved. He had come into an area of unusually tall, straight whitebeech trees, forming a thick canopy overhead. Which meant almost no undergrowth, save for a few tough weeds and small flowers.

Nowhere to hide or shelter . . .

A rustle made him leap with new shock. Dropping to the ground at the base of the tree, he slid into a shallow pit among its thick arched roots. Peering past the roots, heart thumping, he waited to see what new menace had arrived.

But, instead, it was an astonishment. With another rustle of leaves, and a flutter of wings, something small and bright *pink* swooped down to settle on a patch of moss.

CHAPTER 15

Joy and horror

'*Rose!*' In his joy Melleron might have shrieked the name, but instinct turned it into a strangled whisper.

'*There* you are, Melleron,' the little dragon said brightly. 'I've been looking for you *everywhere.*'

'I was going to try to look for *you*,' Melleron babbled, leaping up from among the tree's roots. 'Are you all right? What happened to you? Where's Grit?'

'Grit?' Rose said. 'Oh – he's in the woods somewhere. And I'm *fine*. We were attacked by

Horrimal and his gang, but we got away.'

'I thought you'd been hurt, or killed,' Melleron said breathlessly. 'I saw the signs of a fight . . . and there was blood . . .'

'Not mine, I'm glad to say,' Rose replied, with a sharp laugh. 'But I've been *very* worried. I had no *idea* where you might be, with all those monsters after you.'

'I came across the valley . . .' Melleron began. Then he paused, puzzled. 'How did you know the monsters were after me, Rose?'

She twitched. 'Why, I . . . I know Horrimal and his friends are here in these *woods*, so I imagined they came after you. Probably because you have the *spell-book*.' She peered at him intently. 'You do still have it, don't you, Melleron?'

It seemed an odd question for her to ask just then, Melleron thought, especially in an almost *hungry* tone of voice. She also seemed unconcerned about Grit . . . and she was being generally vague, not like her usual self . . . and the brightness in her eyes looked different somehow . . .

Suspicion growing, he had an idea. 'Don't worry about the book, Rose,' he said. 'Worry about yourself. It's not safe here for someone who's bright *pink* . . .'

Bracing himself, he waited for the explosion, the stream of raging blue fire. But the little dragon merely waved a wing. 'I'll be all right . . .' she began.

Icy fear swept over Melleron, and he took a shaky step back. 'You're *not Rose!*' he gasped, and turned to run.

But not swiftly enough. The false Rose shimmered and became the hooded figure of Saelez, face twisting with fury as he snapped a harsh word.

And as Melleron tried to leap away, a length of the glowing magic cord looped itself around his neck, and dragged him thrashing to the ground.

Saelez's laughter was humourless and bitter. 'Did you think you had killed me, treacherous little slave?' he snarled. 'Or did you merely think you left me powerless when you stole my book?'

Melleron said nothing, struggling helplessly against the cord that tethered him.

'Clearly you forgot about my written *copies* of spells,' Saelez went on. Moving threateningly forward, he pulled a sheaf of papers from within his cloak. 'They have lasted well, so I'm far from powerless.' He stuffed the papers away, his eyes flaming. 'But I want my book, boy! I want it *now!*'

Melleron shrank back. But as Saelez thrust out a bony hand, he was halted by the sound of thudding feet. Horrimal and his five followers, arriving at a run.

'Why have you called us to this place, Saelez?' Horrimal growled. 'We need to get out of these woods. We have seen signs of other monsters . . . many of them . . .'

'I'm sure I saw that Orani, above the trees!' the bulging-eyed creature cried. 'They must be looking for us!'

'Let them look,' Saelez sneered, with a careless wave of his hand.

Horrimal's yellow eyes blazed. 'You may not care,' he rumbled, 'but we do!'

In that moment, no one was looking directly at Melleron. Saelez had turned to glare at Horrimal, and it seemed that the monsters hadn't *noticed* him, for the cord around his neck had pulled him back down among the roots of the great tree.

Stealthily, he drew the spell-book from his shirt. For a moment he thought of using it to free himself – but there was no time to search through it for a suitable spell, and Saelez would certainly see it if he tried. So, instead, he pushed it down as carefully as he could into a dark corner of the shallow pit beneath the roots.

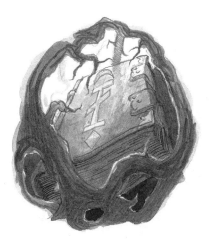

CHAPTER 16

Captives again

'*We* can't turn into birds and fly away!' the purple monster was snarling at Saelez.

'We could all end up in *chains* if they find us!' roared the brown shaggy one.

'They will certainly find you,' Saelez snapped, 'if you go on making so much *noise!*' In the sudden silence, he went on. 'I simply meant that the others will look in vain, because we'll be *gone!*' He pointed. 'I have the boy!'

Horrimal and others looked, and grinned, growling their approval.

'With my spell-book, I can even work a magic

to distract the others,' Saelez went on. He turned to glower at Melleron. 'So, now, boy – give me the book.'

'I don't have it,' Melleron said, letting his voice tremble slightly.

The sorcerer's bony hands curved like talons. 'What do you *mean*, you don't *have* it?' he screeched.

'Not so loud,' whined the bulging-eyed monster nervously.

'I threw it away,' Melleron said. It was almost a whimper, as he slid back into the weak and timid role he had played in the cave. 'In the mountains. I didn't want to carry it. It . . . it scared me.'

Saelez reached out, ablaze with fury. 'It is *I* who should scare you,' he rasped.

Gripping Melleron's shirt-front, he searched him, quickly and roughly – pockets, shirt, trouser legs, anywhere that might be able to hide a thick heavy book.

'So it's true,' he hissed furiously at last. 'The little faint-heart, fearing the book of power, simply threw it away. The most precious object in the world . . .'

'He was not so fearful when he attacked you,' Horrimal rumbled.

'That would have been a sudden impulse,' Saelez sniffed. 'Had he stopped to think, he would have been terrified.'

'So do we twist his neck?' the scaly monster asked hopefully.

'Oh, no,' Saelez snarled. 'We'll take him back to the mountains. Where he can show me the *exact* spot where he threw the book away. Or he will suffer, terribly. As will his *friends*.' He beckoned to the squat hairless monster. 'Show him.'

The hairless one had a large cloth sack slung over his shoulder, which Melleron hadn't noticed. With a grin, the monster dumped its contents on the ground.

Rose and Grit. Tightly bound once again, and gagged, with the glowing cord.

Saelez sneered at Melleron's horrified expression. 'They're unharmed,' he snarled. 'I need them alive for the magics I plan for them.' He turned to Horrimal. 'Now we must hurry. We have to find the book as soon as possible . . .'

'*We?*' Horrimal growled. 'Do you expect us to dig around in the mountains trying to find your book for you?'

'Forget it!' the armoured monster barked. 'We came to go *raiding*, not chasing around after boys and books!'

Saelez looked outraged. 'Fools,' he snapped, 'don't you realize that book is as vital to you as to me? You *need* my magic . . .'

The others growled, Saelez hissed, and in that new outburst of quarrelling none of them, again, was looking at Melleron. Except Rose and Grit, in silent desperation.

Giving them a small tense smile, he reached down to his sock – untouched by Saelez's rough search. Drawing out the slim roll of bark, he almost moaned with relief. All the spells were still there – a few letters slightly faded, but readable.

In a clear, steady voice, he spoke the words that banished the glowing cords.

In the midst of the quarrel Saelez heard him, and spun wildly around. Just as Rose and Grit, freed from their bonds, hurled themselves into battle.

Shrieking, Rose flew at Saelez like a small pink missile, in such a fury that her flame ignited, blasting blue fire at the sorcerer's face.

Howling, Saelez leaped back, tripped, and tumbled into a straggling patch of hookweed.

In the same instant Grit leaped at Horrimal, his growl almost a roar, and sank his diamond teeth into a shaggy ankle. Horrimal bellowed and kicked, shaking Grit off, but the little dog simply lunged at one of the others.

Suddenly all six monsters were in a frantic roaring muddle, stumbling and lurching, crashing into each other, trying to grab Grit or kick him while dodging his teeth, more often grabbing or kicking one another . . .

While Saelez screeched and flailed, trying to free his cloak from the barbs of the hookweed, cowering away from Rose's flame and her swooping raging attacks . . .

And then Melleron dived down into the pit among the roots, snatched up the spell-book, thrust it and the roll of bark into his shirt, and screamed over all the noise.

'Rose! Grit! *Come on!*'

CHAPTER 17

Surrounded

He leaped away, again weaving among the trees at breakneck speed. And Rose and Grit abandoned their battles and joined him, flashing through the woods with the bellowing monsters thundering in pursuit.

But the three friends, far swifter, gained ground on their pursuers, so the bellowing grew more distant. At the same time, the open area among the whitebeeches was giving way to denser, more tangled bush. As they plunged in among the screening brush, Melleron glanced quickly back – and felt a new cold stab of fear.

Some distance behind, a swallow-hawk was swooping among the trees.

But then he stopped, crouching, and looked again. There was something *wrong* with the hawk. It was flying erratically, diving, swerving, flapping . . . And its wings didn't look right, while its tail was mostly missing . . .

'Look,' Melleron whispered to his friends, who had stopped with him. 'Saelez. His shape-changing magic has gone wrong. The copied spells he's using must be starting to fade . . .'

'Rrrr,' Grit growled.

'He says we can escape Saelez *and* the monsters in these thickets,' Rose said.

Melleron nodded. 'We'll swing away to the left, then start making our way out of the woods altogether.' He grinned. 'Wait till I show you my mist-cloud!'

They raced on through the tangled, shadowed undergrowth, twisting and ducking as they fought their way through it as quickly and quietly as they could. But a moment later the thick brush came to a startling end, so that they almost fell out of it. Into a bright open area, a glade where only grass and flowers grew.

And where, on the far side, three monsters were staring at them.

One was squat, hulking, mud-coloured. Another was tall and bony, with enormous clawed hands and feet. And the third was the green thorny one like a walking tree, who had chased Melleron earlier.

Melleron whirled frantically around, looking for escape. But other fearsome shapes were looming at the sides of the glade, while from behind he could hear the growls of Horrimal and his friends, closing in. And then, overhead, the winged cat-like creature appeared, circling menacingly.

They were trapped, surrounded. And despair closed around Melleron's heart as he faced that final crushing defeat.

As he sagged, it was a last unbearable blow when yet another terrifying monster lumbered into the glade. The gigantic one he had seen before, with four arms and great tusks and long trailing yellow hair.

'What's all this, then?' the giant one boomed.

He wasn't looking at Melleron but to one side, at Rose and Grit. And to his utter dazed amazement, Melleron saw that Grit was wagging his tail, while Rose, perched on a tall flower, was smiling.

'It's a long story, Chief,' she said merrily. 'But we're *very* glad to see you.'

That was the moment when Horrimal and his five friends crashed into the glade, growling savagely, fangs bared at the sight of their victims standing in the open, as if giving up. But then

Horrimal and company looked beyond the three friends, and saw the Chief and the others, all around the glade, glaring at them.

Their growling stopped. Horrimal grunted in shock, some of his friends gulped or gasped, the small scaly one turned entirely white. Wheeling frantically, looking for escape, they halted again in new fright – as more big angry monsters barred the way.

The Chief's scowl was terrifying. 'You've caused enough trouble, Horrimal! I've put you in chains before, and I'll do so again! Take them away and bind them!'

Dejected and defeated, Horrimal and his gang were dragged away.

'Here's their sorcerer friend,' said a voice from above. And the winged Orani floated to the ground – with a glitter-eyed swallow-hawk in her claws. 'He doesn't seem able to fly . . .'

But suddenly the hawk shimmered and was Saelez again. Jerking away from Orani, hot-eyed and raging, he whipped out the sheaf of copied spells from his cloak and began to scream harsh words of evil power.

CHAPTER 18

An end to magic

Nothing happened at all.

As the monsters looked astonished, Orani gave a purring laugh. 'It seems he can't do magic any more, either.'

'Um . . .' Melleron said, feeling a little nervous about speaking up. 'His copies of spells are fading, so he can't say them properly. And he doesn't have his spell-book.'

'But I'll find it!' Saelez shrieked. 'And you will all *regret* this when I do!'

'No,' Melleron said, 'you won't find it.' Reaching into his shirt, he brought out the book.

Saelez screeched, in an even more towering fury. 'Treacherous little thief!' he screamed. 'You had it all *along!*' And he flung himself at Melleron.

But Orani and two other monsters held him back, though he fought and howled and raged. While the Chief peered with interest at Melleron.

'You seem to be at the centre of these adventures, young one,' he boomed. 'Most interesting. Considering that you're the first human ever to set foot in our land.'

'If it wasn't for Melleron,' Rose said pointedly, 'Grit and I would be facing a horrible *fate* in the sorcerer's cave.'

A ripple of shock and interest swept through the gathering of monsters. 'That sounds like a story worth hearing, Rose,' Poljon said with a thorny smile.

'You seem to be a most undesirable person, sorcerer,' the Chief boomed, glaring at Saelez. 'Something must be done about you. Perhaps if we *destroy* your magic book, that will put an end to your evil . . .'

Saelez cackled wildly. 'You can't! It's indestructible!'

Melleron sighed, knowing beyond doubt that the Chief was right, that it had to be done. 'No, it isn't,' he said. 'A spell has appeared in the book, showing how to do it. It's very difficult . . .'

'Then it will be far beyond *you*, fool of a boy!' Saelez yelled.

'*But*,' Melleron went on sharply, 'it also showed a *Swifter Way!*'

Sudden fear silenced Saelez, as Melleron turned towards Rose.

'The Swifter Way to destroy the book is easy enough,' he said, 'but I need help to do it. From someone small and *pink* . . .'

Rose leaped into the air, in her berserk storm of fury at the hated word. 'Not pink, not pink, not *pink!*' she shrieked, with blue fire exploding from her mouth.

And Melleron threw the spell-book at her.

The stream of fire struck the book, enveloping it as it fell. And all of them stared, even Rose, her fury forgotten. For instantly the blazing book shrivelled into a cinder, then tore apart into tiny flakes of ash like black snow, drifting away across the glade, vanishing into nothingness.

'Sorry about that word, Rose,' Melleron breathed. 'But that's what was needed. Dragon-fire.'

Saelez was trembling and moaning, staring at his sheaf of papers – every one of which had gone completely blank. Flinging them aside, he turned with a crazed whimpering howl and staggered away into the brush.

'Let him go,' the Chief said hollowly. 'He is no danger now.'

'Time to go home, then,' Poljon said cheerfully.

'Indeed,' the Chief boomed, with a huge smile full of tusks. 'And we'll show Melleron a true monster celebration!'

Melleron blinked, taken aback. 'Thank you,' he said carefully, 'but if you don't mind I'd like to start towards *my* home. It's such a long way, over the mountains . . .'

'Then let's celebrate right here!' Poljon suggested. 'There's lots of food in the woods – and we wouldn't have to wait to hear Rose's story about all this!'

'And then I'll *fly* you home,' Orani said to Melleron with a smile. 'In no time.'

Melleron's eyes widened. 'Won't Nan be amazed . . .' he breathed.

'She'll be too busy being *thrilled* to have you safely home,' Rose said. 'And we'll come *with* you, if Orani will carry Grit as well. We want to *stay* in the Peaceful Forest, for a while yet.'

So all of them, Rose and Grit as well, rushed off to gather things to eat for the celebration. Leaving Melleron in the glade, half-stunned with amazement and delight at how everything had so suddenly been turned around. Then, remembering, he reached into his shirt to bring out the roll of birch-bark.

It was smooth and clean and totally blank. Not a letter, not the tiniest mark, remained of the spells he had written.

He sighed. So I won't be Melleron the Magician after all, he thought. Still, I *was* – for a time . . .

Smiling a wry smile, he tossed the bark aside, and went to join his friends.

About the Author

Whenever I finish a book,
I feel sad. Leaving the
people, the characters of
the book, is like moving
house and leaving
friends behind. And
when I finished a book
about a boy and some
unusual creatures
(*Melleron's Monsters*) I felt especially sad. I'd had
such a good time with them, I didn't want to let
them go.

So I decided to write another book about
them. And although I'm a bit sad again, now
I'm done, I know I can always go back and visit.
Just as you can.

Other Treetops books at this level include:
Melleron's Monsters by Douglas Hill
Swivel-Head by Susan Gates
In the Shadow of the Striker by David Clayton
Sister Ella by Pippa Goodhart
Carnival by Julie Sykes

Also available in packs:
Stage 16 pack E   0 19 919275 8
Stage 16 class pack E   0 19 919276 6